THE MYSTERIOUS CASE OF THE UNIDENTIFIED BODY

WENDY ELMER

authorHOUSE®

AuthorHouse™
1663 Liberty Drive
Bloomington, IN 47403
www.authorhouse.com
Phone: 1 (800) 839-8640

Published by AuthorHouse   06/23/2015

ISBN: 978-1-5049-1868-8 (sc)
ISBN: 978-1-5049-1867-1 (e)

Library of Congress Control Number: 2015909983

Print information available on the last page.

Any people depicted in stock imagery provided by Thinkstock are models, and such images are being used for illustrative purposes only. Certain stock imagery © Thinkstock.

This book is printed on acid-free paper.

CHAPTER 1

On May 1st, 2011 Norman called a meeting with his favorite squad. Robert's squad.

He said: "Good morning gentlemen. We have been asked to spend the summer in Boston, Massachusetts to help solve a case. Your reputation of solving cases has been noticed by other states. The current chief of police used to work as a state trooper unit for the state of Nevada."

John asked: "Where did he work out of?"

Norman said: "He worked out of Eli. He has been in Boston, Massachusetts for about a year now. He is known as a tough old bird, but we can handle him. The cops can respect him and handle him."

Robert asked: "When will we be going?"

Norman said: "We will leave on the fifteenth of the month. The Boston Police Department will pay our hotel bills. We will drive an RV to the city. Our wives and pets will all be going with us. Peter, you will take your Great Danes by your own RV. John you will bring your cat. Robert, bring your Beagle. I am lucky enough not to have any pets."

John asked: "What about paying the rent?"

Norman said: "You will still get Direct Deposit of your paychecks. The Boston police made sure there was a Chase bank where you and your wives can get to. We will be staying at the Four Points Hotel in East Revere. They are pet friendly. John, don't forget to bring your rent envelope for June, July, and August. Notify your landlord to keep an eye on the place. Our approximate return date will be September 1st. Any more questions?" Everybody shook their head no.

Norman said: "Meeting adjourned. Try to finish up whatever you are working on."

John asked: "Wait a minute sir. I just thought of something. What about Commissioner my horse?"

Norman said: "We will not be needing him for this assignment. Since you two are so close I already made arrangements with all parties involved to bring Commissioner with you. He will stay at the horse stables in Boston. I know he keeps you focused. You can go early in the morning to visit him."

John said: Thank you sir." He left with a big smile on his face.

Robert said: "John, go and prepare him for the trip. And no you may not bring him in the RV with you. He will ride in his own truck."

John left and started his shift on the strip.

CHAPTER 2

Everybody ran home and told their wives about the coming adventure. John's wife was so excited about going to Boston. She was even more excited about going on a trip with an RV. That was always her life's dream. John spent the evening notifying the landlord of this development. His landlord gave him 3 self addressed stamped envelops for the rent. He promised to keep an eye on the place. When he got home he checked the supply of checks. The last thing they had to establish was what to do with the bills. The cable and Cong Ed and so forth. John already thought of that and made arrangements to have their mail forwarded to the hotel. Whatever might take too long the landlord would pay himself.

All of the other wives were just as excited. Daisy the Beagel started barking and wagging her tail. Peter's two Great Danes started jumping around and barking too. They loved to slide their nails along the floor. Robert, Peter, and Normal all got ready. The next day the squad went to an

RV dealer and got a good deal. The salesman was a friend of the cops and go them an extra sweet deal. They each had to pay $800.00 plus the cost of gas. They had a crash course on what kind of gas to use and where to put it. All the cops went inside and outside of all the RV's. They looked like kids in a candy store. Each one had a kitchen to cook in and a bedroom. The tricky part was getting the wives not to buy souvenirs at every stop. They each had showers and flushable toilets. The ladies couldn't use it because they needed elbow room in the shower. Females can't potty with the doors open. John wouldn't touch that with a ten foot pole. Every time Michelle got up the cat jumped on her seat and took over. The wives were too excited to see the country to take a nap during the day. They stopped at 5:00 for dinner and stayed wherever they were. Robert had to walk the dog and stretch his legs. All of the dogs needed help getting up and down the stairs. They didn't know what to make of it. Robert had to pick up Daisy and carry her up the stairs.

CHAPTER 3

Finally the big day came and each cop set out early. They had to drive north to Eli and then east onto Route 80. They all stopped at the same hotel each night. Robert and Peter each walked the dogs when they stopped at the hotels. On the road the wives ate like food was going out of style. They carefully picked hotels that had continental breakfasts each morning. They traveled right behind each other. Robert was in the lead because his wife was on the internet to find proper hotels. They all called and texted each other. Then men just followed directions. The men cleverly put a piece of masking tape on the back of the RV's with their names on it. This way if they got separated the drivers would know whom they were following. Each night John walked Commissioner the horse up and down the street and around the hotel. They got a few stares and giggles and a six year old pointed to the horse and started cackling. They all got a kick out of the unusual sight. Commissioner was happy to get the attention. John played with fire and brought the horse into the breakfast room and Norman almost flipped out. John just started laughing and said the horse wanted his morning greeting. Robert calmed down Norman and ordered John to return the horse to the van. He never did that again. John just wanted to start everybody's day with a laugh.

Norman said: "Robert, you better control him!!"

Robert said: "Yes sir. I promise he won't do it again."

Robert ran after them and yelled: "Freeze!!! Both of you!!!"

When they stopped dead in their tracks Robert caught up to them and said: "What in tarnation were you thinking?!!!"

John said: "I was trying to leave a mark on our presence and make people happy and surprise them. It starts their day on the right track and gives them something to talk about."

Robert said: "Four people dropped hot coffee on their laps and three people dropped hot water on themselves. Peter is checking on the women with hot coffee for 2nd degree burns. Luckily nobody has been injured too badly. The women agree to ice cubes on their thighs. Please promise me you won't try another stunt like that again."

John said: "Okay. I promise it won't happen again."

Robert asked: "How did you manage to get the horse in there anyway?"

John said: "We walked in the front door. The clerk weighed barely 120 lbs soaking wet. It was her against a cop and a horse. Who do you think is going to win that competition. She was in such shock all she could do was point. My interest is in getting people start talking. It was so quiet you could hear a roach fart in the back corner of the room. Nobody talks anymore. All people do is vacuum in the food and rush away. Nobody even looks at each other across the table anymore."

Robert said: "I know you have these deep feeling about that, but not in front of the boss. Just behave yourselves in front of Normal. Now go back to the van."

John returned Commissioner and they all had a good laugh for the stunt. He had to be extra careful about what he did the rest of the trip. Commissioner and John bid each other farewell for a while.

CHAPTER 4

The next morning the hotel was a one story affair. All the windows were on ground level. Joyce was getting dressed after her shower. She let out a blood curdling scream. Robert ran out of the shower in the nude and Joyce pointed to the window. There was Commissioner with his nose pressed to the window staring at both of them. Robert dropped to the floor and put a towel around himself to cover up. Joyce threw him a pair of shorts. At breakfast Robert asked John: "What were you doing this morning?"

John said: "Sir. I walked Commissioner and fed and watered him."

Robert asked: "Why was he looking in our window?"

John said: "That was his own doing. You told me yesterday not to bring him into the hotels. I didn't technically."

Robert sent a text to everyone to be ready to check out and leave by 9:00.

Robert asked: "One more thing John. Suppose my wife and
I were making love or in a marital position?"

John said: "Commissioner and I would have turned away. If
you were doing that you should have closed the curtains."

Everybody was on time and did what they were told.
Everybody saw Commissioner and greeted him for the day.
He was very happy to be seen by the cops. He put on his
best face for Norman.

They all left on time and continued on towards Boston.
They ran into traffic at the George Washington Bridge.
They came over and went to the Cross Bronx Expressway.
The sign said I95. Robert was told that that is the right
road. Joyce and Michelle celebrated with a loud yeah!!!
When they hit that road. They stopped in Connecticut
for the night. It was a Holiday Inn. The group got lucky
that they always found nice hotels to stay in. After they
settled in Robert called the Boston sergeant in charge and
was given directions from there. They were expected to
arrive by 1:00 in the afternoon. Robert had to stop once
to get directions. They parked outside South Station
Amtrak station and found their way in. Robert flashed his
badge and explained that they needed directions to the
Four Points Hotel in East Revere. The ladies went to the
restroom while the gentlemen grabbed some lunch. The
directions were perfect. Fairly easy to follow. The accent
was a little hard to understand.

CHAPTER 5

The group arrived at the hotel right at 1:00. They were met by the Boston Chief of Police Jordan Jones. The first day there were introduction all around. Jordan's wife agreed to play tour guide for the ladies. The whole group went to the mall next door. After they checked in they retired to their rooms until dinner. They went next door to the Pizza Uno for dinner. Jordan paid the bill for the first night. Since the next day was Saturday they went to St. Francis of Assisi Church for Saturday Night Mass. Sunday they went to visit Notre Dame Cathedral. Jordan rented a van to fit everybody. The weekend was meant for relaxing after their long trip. The group went to the Boston Commons for shopping. The ladies made a date to go to Cape Cod on Monday. Jordan told his wife to stay as long as they like. The men might be late coming home at night. They needed reassurance that the ladies are safe and sound and in good hands. Once the guys get involved in a case time means nothing to them. Some characteristics of cop life are the same universal. The ladies brought snacks to the room each night. The second night they went to CVS for suntan lotion. They were going to need to slather it on for a long time. Jordan's wife Marisa rented a van for transportation. Before they all piled in Marion reminded them of the seat belt laws applying to the back seat passengers as well. There was no argument on that front.

CHAPTER 6

The ladies arrived on Cape Cod in time for the 11:00 a.m. boat to the other island. They were all told to get out of the van and bring the backpacks and extra weight with them. Michelle almost fainted when she saw the van go straight onto the boat. She had to walk up the stairs to the top deck. Then the horn blew seven times and she got nervous about that. It was obvious she wasn't much of a sailor. She finally settled down after a tod dog and some coffee. They made it to the other end of the island. They took a walking tour with Marisa and she explained about the houses on the island. It was the same island President O'Bama vacationed at. There was one beautiful pink house that looked literally like a doll house. Marisa explained that most of the houses on the island were only summer houses. Only a handful were winterized. They managed to find the shipping area. They stopped in a restaurant for lunch. Joyce paid this time. Michelle left the tip. The ladies managed not to buy anything miraculously. They all returned to the three o'clock boat so the dogs could be walked.

Marisa asked: "Michelle, what time did your husband get up this morning?"

Michelle said: "He got up around 5:00. He had to go and look after Commissioner the horse. Whenever there is not a case John works with Commissioner. They have been inseparable for four years now. John is considered part of the mounted police."

Joyce said: "Michelle, tell Marisa of that stunt he pulled on the road."

Michelle said: "In Las Vegas the cops are always pulling tricks on each other and unsuspecting civilians. John has one issue close to his heart that people don't talk to each other anymore. While on the road we were in the hotel breakfast room and here comes John with Commissioner and saying good morning to everybody. He wanted to give people something to talk about. Norman fell off his chair backwards and four people spilled hot coffee on themselves. Somebody else went around to the ladies and checked out their thighs for burns. Luckily only ice cubes were necessary. The next morning he pulled a fast one on Robert. He had Commissioner press his nose up against the window of his room. Joyce let out a blood curdling screech and Robert ran out of the shower in the nude. He scurried to cover himself. John said: what is the problem? If you were making love you should have closed the curtains."

Marisa said: "Your husband sound like quite a character. Sounds like he keeps the group occupied."

Joyce said: "That he does. He keeps them on their toes. Drives Robert and Norman nuts with his antics. John is the baby of the group, so they all treat him like the son they never had. Sometimes he takes it too far and the squad has to reign him in."

Marisa arrived back at the hotel and they all said good-bye to one another. Naturally they went to the store for evening snacks. They each retired to their own empty room for snack and TV and then sleep. It was a successful day. The wives couldn't wait to share it with their husbands. Too bad they all fell asleep before they got home.

CHAPTER 7

The husbands were picked up that morning at 9:00 a.m. They were all waiting outside when Jordan arrived to pick them up. John was picked up at 6:00 a.m. to take care of Commissioner. His pick-up was named Jeremiah Polinsky. He was driven to the horse stables. Commissioner was taken outside for his walk and fed and watered. He seemed very happy with his new temporary home. Robert promised him that if he was good John would be allowed to take the horse out into the public. After about an hour Jordan showed up to pick up John and start the day. He was ready. John was taken to a prearranged location and met the rest of the team. They were in the precinct gym and were given a sweat suit to wear. Soon all other police officers arrived with the same suit on. The sergeant got on the stage with the microphone and said; "Ladies and gentlemen. We have special visitors with us from the Las Vegas police department. They will help us with our one cold case that we have all been working on."

Jimmy asked: "Which one is that?"

The sergeant said: "You were not in this department when this case came up. It was a headless body and the hands and feet were also cut off. We are trying to identify the body. All we know is that it was a Caucasian male."

Jimmy asked: "How can you tell that without the head?"

The sergeant said: "We took his briefs off and looked at his privates. There are at least 100 people in this room. At least some of us can tell a male from a female. Now everybody dismissed!!"

CHAPTER 8

They adjourned to the sergeant's office. He said: "Please forgive Jimmy. He is like a child."

Norman said: "Don't worry. Our John was the same way. We still have to reign him in at times, but when it comes to following orders he is the one we can rely on. We treat him like the son we never had. I promise that after a year on the job he will settle in."

The sergeant said: "Man I hope so. I don't like being embarrassed in front of visitors."

Norman asked: "Excuse me sir. Why did we put on these sweat suits?"

The sergeant said: "Good heavens. We start each day with 30 minutes of calisthetics, sit ups, and running. Jimmy distracted me and I forgot about the exercises. One of these days I am going to ring that boy's scrawny little neck."

Norman said: "Let me give you a little piece of advice. Never let Jimmy near a horse. Just keep him away from the mounted police squad."

The sergeant said: "I don't know where to take that, but I will take that under advisement. Just promise me one thing. You will all do 30 minutes of exercise tonight."

Norman said: "Absolutely. You have our word on it."

There was a knock on the door and entered was the chief of police Jordan Jones. Everybody stood at attention and saluted as required.

Jordan said: "At ease men. Please be seated." Everybody sat down. They all remembered the posture.

Jordan said: "Ah. I see you met my friends from Las Vegas. Tell me fellows. Has the sergeant been entertaining you properly?"

Robert said: "Yes sir. He has been a perfect gentleman."

Jordan said: "Tomorrow we start work. Everybody be in front of the hotel by 8:00. You will participate in our exercise program every morning. That will be the routine for the duration of your stay with us. Any questions?"

Everybody said in unison: "No sir."

Jordan said: "Very well then. Sergeant, return these men to their hotel."

That was their cue that they were dismissed. That night everyone went to Friendly's restaurant for dinner. The wives joined them.

Norman said: "Wow Paul. He makes me look like a pussy cat. I hope I don't come off like that."

Robert said: "Don't worry Norman. At least you don't set my nerves on edge. One look at that guy and you want to role over and play dead."

Paul asked: "How did he get to make your acquaintance?

Norman said: "We had a missing child case a few years back. He said he was impressed with us. We ended up closing six missing child cases. It was John who cracked it wide open."

Paul said: "He looks and acts rather gruff, but his wife tells me he is totally different at home. He comes home, eats his dinner, does his own thing and then goes to bed. As long as his wife doesn't ask too many questions his is fine with it."

John asked: "Does his wife work?"

Paul said: "Yes. She is a secretary somewhere. Her boss is pretty much the same way. Absentee. He comes in in the early morning and then leaves for the day. If he is in the office at all he is hiding in his office doing paper work.

John asked: "How does she get paid and her timesheet?"

Paul said: "That is done from personnel and payroll. They
do it for the whole firm."

They ordered an ice cream cake for a nightcap. The ladies
already brought the paper plates, napkins, and cutlery.
Paul and his wife were invited, but they politely declined.
Luckily the cake wasn't half melted by the time they got
back to the hotel. The group invaded Robert's room for the
nightcap. He was lucky enough to have a round table as
well as a desk.

When everybody left Robert asked: "Joyce, what are you
   planning for tomorrow?"
Joyce said: "Tomorrow we are planning a tour on a trolley.
   Paul's wife has to work. We already took this tour, but
   there was something else we want to see. We will have
   a picnic at the grave of John Adams."
Robert said: "Good God Joyce!!! Are you ladies insane?
   You want to disturb a president's final resting place by
   eating a bologna sandwich at his grave?"
Joyce said: "No. It is a ham sandwich."
Robert asked: "How will you get there?"
Joyce said: "We will take the hotel van to the train station
   and then take the train. We will redo the route we
   already took last week."
Robert said: "All I can say to that is good luck to you. Don't
   forget the suntan lotion."

Joyce asked: "What time do you want to get up in the morning?"

Robert said: "At 7:00 tomorrow morning. We will grab a bagel on the way out."

CHAPTER 9

The next morning the ladies met downstairs to eat a continental breakfast. Their day went off without a hitch. It took the four of them to put their heads together to navigate the train system. The escalator was a fun ride. The tour guide was a different one than last week, so they heard a different commentary. They got off at stop 6 and walked through the cemetery. It wasn't hard to find the grave of John Adams. The one next to it was Thomas Jefferson. The girls tried to review the story of the Old North Church. Joyce yelled out: "The British Are Coming!!!" They were getting looks from other bystanders. They plopped down and dug into their sandwiches. When they left after about two hours they gathered the garbage and started for the bus stop. They made for the Old North Church and found it. The bus driver directed them up the hill. That was quite a trek. By the time they got there everybody was too tired to kneel or sit, so they stood before the altar and said some prayers for the police department. Joyce lit a few candles and then they left. They made it back to the hotel just in time to walk Daisy. Peter's wife also had to walk the two Great Danes. It was a successful and fun day. When Robert got home Joyce and Daisy were sleeping together in the same bed. He had no choice but to sleep in the other bed.

Michelle on the other hand told John all about their day. She was in awe of being in the Old North Church. They didn't know if it was a Catholic Church or a Protestant Church, but it didn't really matter. It had candles and an altar. The stained glass windows reflected the story of Paul Revere.

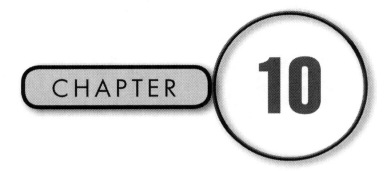

CHAPTER 10

The next morning Joyce woke up and felt bad that she was sleeping when Robert came home. Robert and Joyce went down to breakfast together and Norman joined them. His wife slept in. She was never an early riser.

Norman asked: "How are you enjoying your first visit to Boston?"

Joyce said: "I am enjoying it very much. The people here are so friendly and helpful to visitors. On the train there is always some employee there to help you. I was appointed group leader for the wives."

Norman asked: "What did you think of The Old North Church?"

Joyce said: "I kind of felt sorry for the horse who had to drag his hooves up the hill. That must have been murder on his feet. One thing I couldn't tell is if it was a Protestant or Catholic or a Presbyterian Church. I really couldn't tell."

Norman said: "Let me clear that up for you. The Protestant churches don't have the Corpus on the Cross. The Catholics do have that. What are you doing today?"

Joyce said: "I think first I will take Daisy for a walk and then take it from there."

Robert said: "I think we need to stroll outside now."

Norman said: "One question Robert. Did you see our son today?"

Robert said: "No sir. He leaves before I wake up. I don't hear him leave, so he probably tip toes down the hall."

Norman said: "Good day Joyce. Robert, let's go find everybody and gather together."

They left and found John outside already doing exercises. Norman and Robert joined him in the act of jumping jacks. John's wife told him that jumping jacks hurts her chest flopping up and down like that. He surprised everyone by getting really interested in morning exercises. The other two members hated the morning exercises. You needed a cattle prod to get them out of bed.

When they finished Norman asked about Commissioner. John reported he is happy and healthy and glad for his temporary home. They took their morning constitution early before anybody got up.

CHAPTER **11**

The group of cops was picked up outside the hotel right on time. They were taken to the local precinct meeting room. They were welcomed by Paul. John was already there with a big smile on his face. He was very excited to be in Boston. He never traveled much that he remembered. He couldn't help comparing his precinct with the one in Boston. Both rooms had no windows.

Paul said: "Here we go. These pictures are rather graphic and I hope you don't have a weak stomach." He opened the folder and passed around the pictures. John ran out of the room and threw up.

Norman said: "Sorry about that Paul. He is our best puzzle solver. I promise he will come around."

John reentered the room and apologized for his reaction. He promised to get it together.

Paul said: "What can you tell us about solving this case? You were brought in here because you have a reputation for doing the impossible."

Robert asked: "When did this occur?"

Paul said: "This happened two years ago."

Robert asked: "Where did this occur?"

Paul said: "It occurred in Paul Revere park."

John asked: "Whatever happened to the rest of the body?"

Paul said: "He is in the city morgue in a refrigerator all by himself."

John asked: "Did you do DNA testing on the hair?"

Paul said: "Without the head we have no hair."

John said: "Ordinarily that would be true. I am wondering about the public hair."

Paul said: "His pubic hair was shaved shortly before his death. In fact his whole body was shaved."

John said: 'We probably have a repeat offender here. Somebody that is familiar with morgue and police procedures. Probably somebody who watches Law and Order. This way he doesn't have to be an outsider."

The door opened and a gurney came in. The carcass was under the sheet. John took one look at it and found hair on the body. It was just peach fuzz, but it was something. The Boston cops didn't know that after death the hair keeps growing. The pathologist was told to take a piece of hair and put it into the DNA database. The only thing that would tell you is if he was a criminal. If he had no record there still won't be a name.

Paul asked: "How are we going to get an identification on the head?"

John said: "That is easy. Take a tape measure and measure the neck, wrists and ankles. We will fax these measurements to our office in Las Vegas. We have a guy who can make a computer image of the head. We will have to guess at the hair color and eye color, but it should be pretty close. It will be a start."

Paul said: "Thank you John. We will try this then."

The cops waited until the next day to get the measurements. The pathologist couldn't find a tape measure, so it took longer than necessary. He finally wrote down the measurements and handed them off to Paul. They called it a day and went home. It was all too much to handle in one day. They were driven home because they all looked like they were going to pass out. When they got to the hotel the cops sat on the grass and stayed there until the color came back into their faces. They were told to hold their heads down toward their knees. When the escorts left the guys went to CVS for ginger ale to settle their stomachs. Robert ended up taking a nap because he was exhausted.

CHAPTER 12

The next day the cops gathered at Paul's office and John was given the paper. He needed Peter's help to work the fax machine. Robert got a phone call from the office about this new assignment. The officer said it would take at least 24 hours to get a good picture. He will fax the picture as soon as possible. The rest of the day the boys spent the day sight seeing because there was nothing more to be done. Paul was upset about giving the boys the day off, but he couldn't help it. They were driven back to the hotel where they went to Burlington Coast Factory to shop. John and Robert never knew that the store sold men's clothes. They surprised their wives by springing money for the evening snacks. They all decided to go to McDonalds's for dinner that night. While at McDonald's Robert received a text that said they will fax the images right away. The identification shouldn't take much longer. Paul told them that unfortunately the cops would have to stick around for the trial if there was one. The wives weren't too happy with that, but they went along wit it anyway. They had no choice. Only the men knew how to drive an RV. John told Robert to release the images on the news. That would generate a lot of tips.

Robert said: "I will relay that to Paul tomorrow."

That night Robert snored so loudly that Norman heard him all the way through the walls. He had an idea to order his adenoids removed. They had talked about it before, but Robert said that was already done. It did nothing for his snoring. Norman asked Joyce about Robert's snoring. She said that sometimes she has to sleep on the couch to get away from it. Luckily she sleeps in the hospital 3 times a week. Joyce told Norman that Robert only snores like that when he is on a case. Poor Daisy had no choice but to stay and she had no place to escape to. At least at home she can go and hide in the bathroom.

CHAPTER 13

Day 4 of the visit started out like any other. The cops gathered in Paul's office for their morning meeting.

Robert said: "Paul, John had an idea last night. He said you should show the picture on the news and details of whom this person is or was as whatever the case may be."

Paul said: "We will call a news conference this afternoon at 3:00 in the gymnasium. You guys will stand behind me. I will do all the talking. Please go back to the hotel and put on your suits and ties. You will be picked up at 2:30 for your return. Wear your guns and badges."

Paul's cell phone rang and he hit pay dirt. There was a positive ID on the body based on the computerized image and missing person's bureau. Paul sent two detectives to the man's family to inform them of his death. The next step was the investigation as to how he ended up like that and who did it to him. The man's family wanted his organs donated, but unfortunately that wasn't an option because he had been dead for too long.

By 2:00 half the auditorium was filled with microphones, wires, and every other thing under the sun imaginable. Everybody was testing out the microphones and the video cameras were everywhere with more people wearing headphones and getting angle shots. At a quarter to three Robert and his squad arrived at the precinct. They were led to the gymnasium and onto the stage. They had to be careful of where they were stepping. Naturally Robert and Norman both tripped on the way up the stairs. As soon as they got on stage the flashes started going off. Robert whispered to John to relax and not freak out over the flashes. At precisely 3:00 Paul took the stage.

He said: "Good afternoon everyone. Thank you for coming out on such sohort notice. On July 1st, 2013 a body was found at Paul Revere Park. The body had no head, face, or feet or hands. We had no way of figuring out who he was. We sought the help of the Las Vegas Police Department Detectives and they helped us through this puzzle. All we knew was that the victim was male. He had no body hair. Luckily his private areas was still in tact. He had no breasts. He has been positively identified as 30 year old Joshua Mitchell. The head, feet, and hands have never been found. The body will be in Flynn Funeral Home on Tuesday and Wednseday from 1:00-5:00 and 7:00-9:00. He was unemployed at the time of his disappearance. For obvious reasons the coffin will be a closed coffin. The body has been washed and he will be buried in his tuxedo. He was engaged to be married next year. His funeral Mass will be in Notre Dame Cathedral on Thursday at 10:00. It will be open to the public. Now we are asking the public's help in figuring out who did this. On the screen you will see a picture of Jacob. If anybody was in Paul Revere Park on June 30th, 2013 and you remember him please call the tip line. The number is on your screen. We are also talking to family members who knew him best. If you have any video tapes from that day and he appears in it in the background please turn the tapes over to the police. We promise to take good care of them. You have our word of honor that they will not be gawked at or laughed at. We will return the tapes to you undamaged as soon as possible. Our goal right now is to put together his last hours of his life. We also might see the killer on the tape. Thank you for your help."

As he was talking the tip line lit up like a Christmas Tree. The poor police department had to ferret out the legitimate tips from the not so legitimate ones. It would be a very long night for the police department. The boys offered to help, but the Boston Police turned them down. Paul said that too many people on one job would create confusion.

CHAPTER 14

The next night the cops showed up at the wake. They were milling around outside the funeral home. The cops looked at the tapes and stood inside and had technology attached to the bushes. They tried facial recognition technology. They put everybody's picture in the computer and everybody who walked in front of the camera had his picture taken. They got these pictures from the background of the tapes. There was also a cloth picked up and preserved at the scene. There was a body and crime sniffing dog at the wake. Nobody knew about the clothes left at the scene. Sure enough one person entered and the dog barked. The cop at the door stopped him and asked if he would accompany him to the police command center. He readily agreed. He had his picture taken again. The cops put it in the computer again and came up with a match.

Paul asked: "What is your name?"

He said: "My name is Victor James."

Paul asked: "How did you know the victim?"

Victor said: "He was on my little league baseball team."

Paul asked: "The victim's name was Chester Mansfield. What kind of person was he?"

Victor said: "Chester was a team player. He was willing to do anything for anyone."

Paul asked: "When was the last time you saw Chester?"

Victor said: "I last saw him at the championship game in 2003."

Paul asked: "Who was the coach of the team?"

Victor said: "The coach's name was Luke Mansfield."

Paul asked: "What kind of relationship did you have with Luke the coach?"

Victor said: "There weren't any problems. We did everything we were told."

The dog started growling by the front door and showing his fangs. He wasn't going to let Victor leave the van without being in handcuffs. The dog was given the command to smell the evidence and then he smelled Victor's crotch. The dog sat and that was the signal for a match.

Paul said: "Victor, you are under arrest for the murder of Chester Mansfield. You have a right to remain silent. You have the right to an attorney. If you cannot afford one one will be appointed for you. Do you understand these rights as I have read them to you?"

Victor said: "Yes. But may I ask one thing of you?"

Paul said: "Okay. What is it?"

Victor said: "I would like to go inside and pay my respects to the widow."

Paul said: "Okay. I will bring you inside wearing handcuffs. I will uncuff you just long enough to bless yourself and say your prayers. You can shake hands with the mother, but then I have to put the cuffs back on. One false move and my dog will hear you to pieces. Do you understand?"

Victor said: "Crystal clear sir. I promise not to give you a hard time. Not with that dog anyway."

They all marched inside and Victor knelt down and apologized to the dead person for what happened. The cops stood behind him and the dog stood next to Paul at alert attention. He wouldn't take his eyes off of Victor for any reason.

Chester's mother asked: "Why are you in handcuffs Victor?"

Paul answered for him and said: "He admitted to doing this heinous act. The killer left behind his shirt and we never release that information. My dog sniffed the shirt and then Victor's crotch. It was a definite match. He will be arraigned in criminal court tomorrow morning. Then comes the trial."

Amanda asked Victor: "You honestly did this to my son?"

Victor said: "Yes. I did. I don't remember the act, but it is
looking like it."

Amanda beat her fists against his chest and told the cops
to get him out of here. They left without further incident.

CHAPTER 15

Victor was taken to the police station for questioning. Because of the late hour he was questioned for about an hour and then put in a cell all by himself. He was offered dinner, but he accepted just coffee and a few cookies.

Paul asked: "What is your full name?"

Victor said: "My name is Victor James."

Paul asked: "Did you perform this heinous act?"

Victor said: "Yes. I beheaded him and cut off his hands and feet."

Paul asked: "Why did you do that?"

Victor said: "Because he raped my sister."

Paul asked: "Why didn't you cut off his private parts?"

Victor said: "I left his privates, but he was alive when I cut off his hands and feet. I wanted him to suffer as much as possible."

Paul asked: "What did you do with his head, hands, and feet?"

Victor said: "I put them in a plastic bag with a magnet and threw them into the St. Charles river. I knew they wouldn't surface with the magnet in the bag."

Paul asked: "What kind of work did you do?"

Victor said: "I am unemployed at the moment."

Paul asked: "Did Chester get arrested and charged with your sister's rape?"

Victor said: "Yes. I knew he had a police record. That is why I had to cut off his hands. His fingerprints are in the system."

Paul asked: "Is your sister still alive to testify?"

Victor said: "No. I blame Chester for her suicide."

Paul asked: "When did this suicide take place?"

Victor said: "A week before this happened was the funeral."

Paul asked: "What kind of knife did you use?"

Victor said: "It was more like a rotary drill with teeth."

Paul asked: "How long was Chester's jail sentence?"

Victor said: "He was let off on a technicality. The arresting officer forgot to read him his rights. That is when I went over the edge. My sister was pregnant from the rape. We were planning on keeping the baby. I was going to play the role of the kid's father."

Paul asked: "Was she carrying a boy or a girl?"

Victor said: "We couldn't tell yet. The pregnancy wasn't that far along."

Paul asked: "How did your sister commit suicide?"

Victor said: "She hung herself in her bedroom."

Paul asked: "Where did you do the killing itself?"

Victor said: "It was done at Thomas Jefferson Park. I drove him over to Paul Revere park."

Paul asked: "How did you get rid of all the blood?"

Victor said: "Lestoil, Clorox, and Kaboom. All three of those cleaners were used. It all worked. There wasn't a trace of blood left."

Paul said: "While we were sitting here my team went to your apartment and found there was a bloodbath in your apartment and car. How did the blood get into your apartment?"

Victor said: "I brought the rags home that I used to clean my car. I guess it was transported that way."

Paul said: "This afternoon you will be brought to the courthouse for arraignment. That is where you will plead either guilty or not guilty. You will meet your lawyer before that. Your lawyer will do all the talking. You just stand there and keep silent. Do you have any questions?"

Victor said: "No sir. I am relieved that this is coming out. I do have one question though. How did you find the blood in my apartment?"

Paul said: "That is easy. We luminal everything. It is standard procedure.

CHAPTER 16

The prosecutor's name was Jacques Strauss. The lawyer's name was Charles Weinstein. At precisely 2:00 Victor was brought over to the courthouse for arraignment.

Judge Cressler said: "Victor, you are being charged with murder in the first degree. How do you plead?"

Charles said: "My client pleads guilty your honor."

Judge Cressler asked: "Jacques, what do you want to do?"

Jacques said: "Remand your honor. The defendant butchered a man and withheld information for a year. This man could have been buried a year ago and brought closure to the family. He chose not to."

Judge Cressler asked: "Charles, how do you respond?"

Charles said: "Your honor. My client is a productive member of society. He is willing to surrender his passport to guarantee his appearance at his next court date."

Judge Cressler said: "Very well Charles. Victor will also wear an ankle bracelet. He is to only leave the house for work and then back home. Charles will escort you to work and back home again. Show up back here on Sept. 1ˢᵗ for jury selection. Be here at 9:00 a.m."

Charles said: "Thank you your honor."

Outside the courtroom Charles told Victor he had better play by the judge's rules. He has the reputation of locking people up for the slightest infarction. He was fitted for the ankle bracelet and the rules were explained specifically. Charles escorted Victor home. The phone was required and tested. The court officers didn't leave until they were satisfied that the ankle bracelet was in proper working order.

CHAPTER 17

The whole month before Sept. 1st Victor never once stepped out of line. He took the judge's orders very seriously. He had no choice. Charles was practically glued to him at the hip. They entered the courtroom right at 9:00. The jury was selected the day before. Nobody tried to get out of it. The judge in this courtroom was named Eric Jamison.

Eric said: "Good morning ladies and gentlemen. The case we are hearing will not take too long. You will not be sequestered. I personally dob't believe in that. You will hear opening statements from the prosecutor and the defendant's attorney. They have been instructed to keep their statements short and to the point. You will not hear ridiculous questions irrelevant to this case. The lawyers have nothing to gain or lose whether he is found guilty or not guilty. It makes no difference to them. They do not get any monetary bonus for sending someone to jail. With that I call upon Charles to start the proceedings. Charles, you may begin when ready."

Charles got up and said: "Good morning ladies and gentlemen. My name is Charles Weinstein. I am the defendant's lawyer. That means my job is to convince you not to convict my client. My client pled guilty but it is the why he did it that will come out during testimony. When you hear the why I am sure you will let him go home back to his family. Right now I have to be glued to him and his family is tired of looking at me. I am starting to wear out my welcome. Even if he is sent to jail I will not have to stay in his house. Thank you."

Eric said: "Jacques, please begin your opening statements."

Jacques got up and said: "Thank you Eric. Ladies and gentlemen of the jury. Victor has already pleaded guilty to these charges. The heinous act he committed is unforgivable. He had no business cutting off the head of the victim. I am asking you to let him off because he have lived with this on his conscience for a year now. He had second thoughts after he did it. Another reason I want you to let him off is because you should look into your own souls and see how you would react. True he could have turned himself in, but he was arrested and found not guilty. There is no way of knowing if he butchered the right man. There is no proof anymore. Thank you your honor."

Eric said: "Ladies and gentlemen of the jury. Because of the late hour we will be dismissed for the day. Everybody return here by 9:00 tomorrow morning and we will begin. I promise it will not take too long. Bailiff, please escort the jury out. The defendant will remain here until the bailiff returns."

With that the jury was led out of the courtroom. The bailiff returned about 5 minutes later. Victor was escorted home still wearing the ankle bracelet that would remain on him until the end of the trial. It was a relief to be home from court. His wife greeted him at the door. His kids were glad to see him.

CHAPTER **18**

Day 2 of the trial started right on time. Nobody was late. The jury knew they would be in trouble if they were late.

The bailiff yelled: "ALL RISE!!!" Everybody rose as instructed.

Eric walked in ad said: "You may be seated." Everybody sat on cue.

Eric said "Charles, you may begin with your first witness."

Charles got up and said: "Thank you your honor. I call Robert Shapiro to the stand."

Robert stood up, straightened his tie and approached the stand. The bailiff swore him in and he took his seat.

Charles asked: "Robert, how did you get involved in this case?"

Robert said: "My squad and I are detectives from the LasVegas Police Department. Your chief of police is a former detective with the Eli, Nevada police department. He got involved with one of our cases a few years ago. He was impressed with our skills for solving mysteries. It was John who actually cracked the case. Your chief of police was impressed with our performance. We were called in as consultants for help."

Charles asked: "How long did it take you to solve this case?"

Robert said: "Maybe about a week or so."

Charles asked: "How long did it take you to solve this case?"

Robert said: "Maybe about a week or so."

Charles said: "No more questions your honor."

Eric said: "Jacques, do you have any questions for this witness?

Jacques said: "Yes your honor. Now Robert, how long did it take you to pin this on my client?"

Robert said: "I believe I just answered that."

Eric said: "Wake up Jacques and pay attention. Charles just asked that. Now move on."

Jacques said: "Sorry your honor. May I ask for a continuance?"

Eric asked: "Why Jacques?"

Jacques said: "My mother is in the hospital and my mind is a little distracted today."

Eric asked: "Does she live with you?"

Jacques said: "No sir. She lives out of state. My sister called me this morning and told me. Every time something happens you always think the worst. My sister goes to pieces every time she sneezes and sometimes I have to calm her down."

Eric said: "Very well Jacques. Step back to your seats. Ladies and gentlemen. We will adjourn for the day. By tomorrow Jacques will be paying attention and back into the action."

He hammered his gavel and dismissed the jury.

The bailiff yelled: ALL RISE"

Everybody rose and left the courtroom. The jury left with a smile on their face.

Some of them walked around the mall. They got a good lunch at the food court. Others just went home to stare at the TV.

CHAPTER 19

Day 3 of the trial started right on time.

The bailiff yelled "ALL RISE" The jury rose and the judge entered. The bailiff yelled 'You may be seated!!!" Everybody sat on cue.

The judge said: "Good morning everyone. Jacques, I am
     sure you are prepared today?"
Jacques said: "Yes sir. My head is clear today."
The judge said: "Good. Charles, call your first witness
     please."
Charles said: "I call Norman to the stand."

Norman approached the stand and took the oath of promise to tell the truth, the whole truth and nothing but the truth.

Charles said: "Norman, please tell us your full name for
     the record."
Norman said: "My name is Norman Connor. I am of Irish
     descent."

Charles asked: "How did you get involved in this case?"

Norman said: "I am the chief of police for the Las Vegas Police Department. The Chief of Police for the Boston, Massachussetts police department is a former police officer of Ely Nevada. Our paths crossed and he reached out to us for help."

Charles asked: "How did you get here?"

Norman said: "We all rented RV's and drove out here. Some of us have pets and we didn't want to stress them out. In an RV they were free to roam around."

Charles asked: "Will you be relocating here and leaving Las Vegas?"

Norman said: "No. We will be leaving for home as soon as the trial is over."

Jacques said: "Objection your honor.!!"

Eric asked: "What is your problem Jacques? Counsel approach."

Jacques said: "We seem to be asking the same questions of everyone. We don't seem to be getting anywhere."

Eric said: "I agree. Tomorrow you will ask different questions."

Charles said: "Okay your honor. Point taken."

Eric said: "Ladies and gentlemen. We will adkourn for lunch. Everybody return in one hour for the afternoon session.

At the end of lunch everybody returned right on time.

Eric entered and the bailiff yelled: "ALL RISE!!"

Eric said: "Jacques, you may begin."

Jacques said: "Thank you your honor. Norman, why do you suppose it took a year to identify this victim?"

Norman said: "He had no head, hands, or feet. There was no way of getting a DNA

Sample from him. Even if we had a DNA sample we could only use it if he ahd a police record and his prints were in the system."

Jacques asked: "Why were you so sure the victim was a male and not a female?"

Norman said: "The male anatomy was still in tact. It was obvious once we looked at his privates."

Jacques said: "No more questions your honor."

Eric said: "Very well., You may tep down Norman. Because of the late hour we will adjourn for the day. Have a good evening everybody."

CHAPTER 20

D ay 4 of the trial started right on time.

Eric said: "Charles, please call your first witness."
Charles said: "I call John to the stand."

As John approached he was sworn in as the witness.

Charles asked: "What is your full name for the record?"
John said: "My name is John McFadden."
Charles asked: "What is your reputation with the police
    deparment?"
John said: "I am like the son they never had. I can be a
    bumbling idiot, but they take it all in stride. I have
    never broken a rule. The other guys look out for me and
    make sure I stay out of trouble."
Charles asked: "How long did it take you to climb the ranks
    of the police department.?"

John said: "About a year. They put me on horse training duty. I just did what I was told. The rest of the department also treast me like the son the never had."

Charles asked: What made you want to become a cop?"

John said: "After I got out of jail I met Robert in a supermarktet. I excelled in everything. My career just took off from there. I had no idea I had all these skills inside me."

Charles asked: "Did you bring your horse to Boston?"

John said: "Yes. I brought him with me. He keeps me grounded and my head focused. I did try something bizarre coming over here. I thought Norma was going to drop a baby."

Charles asked: "What did you do to get Norman all excited?"

John said: "We were in the hotel breakfast room having a continental breakfast. I brought my horse into the hotel breakfast room and introduced Commissioner to everyone."

Charles asked: "What reaction did you get?

John said: "Two ladies dropped hot coffee on their laps and one dropped hot eggs on her lap. Luckily nobody was hurt too badly."

Charles asked: "What on earth possessed you to do that?"

John said: "With the dawning of e-mail and face book nobody talks to each other anymore. I did it to get people talking. People sit at the same table and only look at their food. They shove it in their moth and swallow. They don't even look at each other anymore."

Charles asked: "What make you so upbeat?"

John said: "I spend an hour a day reading. I missed reading in jail."

Charles asked: "What were you in jail for?"

John said: "Armed robbery. Nobody got injured but I went to jail anyway. It is all in my past. Nobody holds anything against me. I spend every day of my life impressing people."

Charles said: "No more questions your honor."

Eric said: "Jacques, do you have any questions for this witness?"

Jacques said: "Yes your honor. Now John, how did you happen to conclude that my client did the deed of killing this person?"

John said: "The Boston Police Department had a piece of pant leg from the perp. At the wake we had dogs who sniffed the people as they entered Sure enough the dog gave us a clue that there was a match. We let the defendant go up and pay his last respects to the deceased and family and then we can go outside and talk. We explained that he was not under arrest and he had the right to leave. He chose not to walk away."

Jacques asked: "What was his response when he finished?"

John said: "He seemed relieved that this was off his chest. He never gave us a bit of trouble. He was very cooperative."

Jacques asked: "What excvuse did he give for doing this?"

John said: "He said he raped his sister. He was willing to raise this child as his own, then they met again."

Jacques asked; "Why didn't he just cut off his privates?"

John said: "He said he wanted him to suffer like his sister did."

Jacques asked: "Will you be staying here in Boston permanently?"

John said: "No. We will be returning to Las Vegas as soon as the verdict come in. We want to see this through till the end."

Jacques said: "No more questions your honor."

Eric said: "You may step down John. Ladies and gentlemen of the jury. We will adjourn for the day. Please return tomorrow morning by 9:00 for the trial to continue. Good night all."

With that the jury was escorted out of the building. The defendant was asked to remain until all the jurors were out of the building. The defendant was then escorted back home by his lawyer.

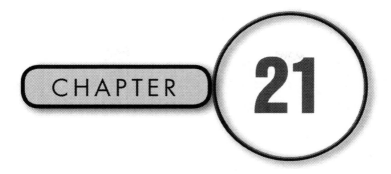

CHAPTER 21

The next day in chambers Eric asked: "Are you guys almost finished?"

Charles and Jacques both said they were almost finished. When they entered the courtroom the bailiff yelled: "ALL RISE!!" Everybody rose and took their seats.

Eric said: "Charles, call your next witness please."

Charles said: "I call Jordan James to the stand."

As Jordan approached he was sworn in as the next witness.

He said: "State your full name for the record."

Jordan said: "My name is Jordan James."

Charles asked: "What is your occupation?"

Jordan said: "I am the chief of police"

Charles asked: "Are you a native Bostonian?"

Jordan said: "No sir. I am not."

Charles asked: "Where are you from originally?"

Jordan said: "I am from Nevada, Carson City specifically."

Charles asked: "What made you move to Boston?"

Jordan said: "I was always attracted to the city of Boston. When the opportunity came up I applied for the job as chief of police and got it. I now have the whole police department under me and answering to me."

Charles asked: "What made you call for help in solving this case?"

Jordan said: "It has been about a year since this person was found. I don't like open cases. It was high time it was solved once and for all. This person had a family that had no closure for a whole year. That was unacceptable in my book."

Charles asked: "How did you learn of the cops in Las Vegas?"

Jordan said: "A few years ago we crossed paths on a case involving Las Vegas police. They came up to Eli and we found the missing child. I was impressed with the squad and knew if anybody could solve this case they can."

Charles asked: "What made you move to Boston?"

Jordan said: "I searved in the navy here in Nantucket. When this job opportunity came up went for it. I got lucky."

Charles said: "No more questions your honor."

Eric said: "Jacqes, do you have any questions for this witness?"

Jaques stood up and said: "Yes your honor. Now Jordan, what contributions have you made to the Boston Police Department?"

Jordan said: "When I first move dhere I was taken around on a listening tour. I noticed that most of the cops were out of shape and sloppy looking. They had pot bellies sticking out so it looked like they were nine months pregnant. I almost asked one guy when was the baby due. That is when I imposed the mandatory 1 hour of exercise before their shift. I make them jog through main street and show off what they look like. I cut short of imposing a weight limit."

Jacques asked: "What is your goal in doing this?"

Jordan said: "My goal is to shame them into getting in shape. How will they catch a thief if they can't move with their guns around their waists? It adds about 15 lbs. to your body weight. They have to run with all that gear on."

Jacques said: "No more questions your honor."

Eric said: "You may step down Jordan. We will adjourn for the day. Have a good evening."

The bailiff yelled: "ALL RISE!!" Everybody rose and left the courtroom.

CHAPTER 22

The Las Vegas detectives were driven back to the hotel. John asked: "Robert, what did Charles mean when he asked me if we were staying?"

Norman said: "Don't be upset about that. He is just trying to rattle your cage. All lawyers do that."

The wives came in and were shocked to see the squad already home.

Robert said: "We are home early today. To celebrate us guys will be taking you ladies to the movies. Then we will spring for evening snacks. The trial is almost over and we will be returning home soon. We want to make it some sort of relaxation. Jordan and his wife came by and offered to drive them to the movies. The trial was expected to wrap up soon. Jordan wanted to leave the cops with a good impression of him. They decided to see The King's Speech. It was an excellent movie. Everybody loved it. The women had to oogle over the acting and John mentiond he expected to see the King projectile vomit through the screen. John was deathly afraid of the elevator in the therapist's office. He wanted to hurdle at the thought of it. Coming back they had to take the long way around because of the rules of the road. They drove 2 miles out of their way to the roundabout and come back again. Just when they got there the gentlemen heard a motor bike speeding out of nowhere. A car came and smashed into him at full force. It looked like a deliberate hit. Jordan jumped out and opened the trunk. He pulled out the cones and placed them on the road. Jordan't wife called 911 to get help. John ran out to check on the driver of the car and Robert ran out to check on the motorcyclist. He was dead on impact. The driver of the car sat there in shock and he looked like he was going to pass out in shock. Between sobs he managed to say he never saw the motorcyclist. The driver turned out to be an observer of the court room of the trial. He was not charged with anything. A Boston police car showed up and he drove the driver home. No charges were ever brought against him, but the shock made him never drive again. It took an hour to clean up the mess. By the time the group got back to the hotel it was too late for snacks. The bid each other a good evening and departed straight for bed.

CHAPTER 23

The next day the court convened at 9:00.

Eric said: "Good morning everyone. Charles, call your first witness please."

Charles said: "I call Victor to the stand." As Victor approached he was sworn in as the next witness.

Charles asked: "What is your full name?"

Victor said: "My name is Victor James."

Charles asked: "How did you know the deceased?"

Victor said: "I first met him as a child. He was my baseball coach."

Charles asked: "How old were you then?"

Victor said: "I was ten years old."

Charles asked: "How did you meet up with him again?"

Victor said: "He went to school with my sister. He raped her. I wasj just going to play daddy with her and pretend I was the father. She identified him. I followed him for a few weeks and got to know his schedule. Then I made my move. He had a pretty regular schedule, so it was easy."

Charles asked: "Did he harm you as a child?"

Victor said: "Yes. He raped me too. I thought he was okay, but years later I learned what he did was wrong. He told me it was okay because he was an adult."

Charles asked: "What did he do to you specifically?"

Victor asked: "Do I have to actually state it?"

Charles said: "Yes. You must name it. Give it words."

Victor said: "He used his tongue on my private area. He also touched me down there."

Charles asked: "Did you tell him to stop?"

Victor said: "Of course I did. What do you think? I may have been just ten, but I knew bad touches from good touches."

Charles asked; "Did you tell anyone?"

Victor said: "No."

Charles asked: "Why not?"

Victor said: "I was too ashamed. He said everybody has it done and it was nothing to be ashamed of."

Charles asked: "Were there any other victims?"

Victor said: "I don't know for sure, but it wouldn't surprise me."

Charles asked: "Have you spoken to other members of the team?"

Victor said: "Only at the funeral. After I left the team nobody talked to me again."

Charles asked: "Do you remember a kid by the name of Jasper Thompson?"

Victor said: "I don't think so. Not off hand anyway."

Charles asked: "Were you friendly with any of the team mates?"

Victor said: "I don't remember for sure. I was just ten years old."

Charles said: "I am prepared to call Jaspter to the stand to testify against you."

Jacques said: "Objection your honor! This witness was not on our witness list."

Eric said: "Approach you two."

Jacques said: "Your honor. Why are we just hearing about this now?"

Charles said: "This witness was only just yesterday made available."

Jacques said: "How do we know he is not just trying to get into the act?"

Eric said: "You don't. But I will allow it. Now step back."

Charles said: "No more questions your honor."

Eric asked: "Jacques, do you have any questions for this witness?"

Jacques said: "Yes your honor. Victor, do you regret what you did?"

Victor said: "Not at all. He did something horrendous and didn't deserve to live. He needed to pay the price."

Jacques asked: "Would you do it again?"

Victor said: "Absolutely."

Jacques said: "No more questions your honor."

Eric said: "You may step down Victor. Ladies and gentlemen of the jury, you are dismissed for the day. Return here tomorrow by 9:00 a.m. Have a good evening all."

The bailiff yelled: "ALL RISE!!" The jury rose and left the courthouse.

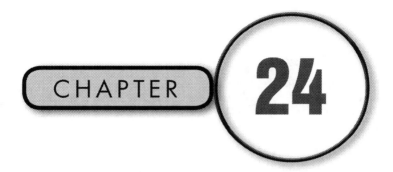

CHAPTER 24

At 9:00 the next morning everybody returned and the trial resumed. Eric entered nad the bailiff yelled "ALL RISE!!!" Everybody rose and the jury was told to be seated."

Eric said: "Charles, call your next witness please."
Charles said: "I call Jasper Thompson to the stand."

As Jasper approached he was sworn in as the next witness.

Charles said: "State your full name for the record."
Jasper said: "My name is Jasper Thompson."
Charles asked: "How did you know the defendant?"
Jasper said: "We played on the same baseball team together.
    Victor did this community a great service by killing the
    coach like he did. He also did the same thing to me."
Charles asked: "Why do you want to come forward now?"
Jasper said: "To support Victor."
Charles asked: "Did you tell anyone?"

Jasper said: "No. I was too ashamed and it all came back to me. I heard it on the news and that got me thinking about it again.

Charles asked: "Where have you been living?"

Jasper said: "My family moved to New York after it happened. I thought I was safe. That is why I never told anyone. I was also afraid of what my father would do to him. I lost interest in baseball after that. My parents thought it was just a phase. They never questioned why I lost interest. My mother put it down as just part of the move and that I was entering a new phase in life. She got it half right."

Charles said: "No more questions your honor."

Eric said; "Jacques, do you have nay questions for this witness?"

Jacques said: "Yes your honor. Is Jasper your given name or a nickname?"

Jasper said: "No. It is a nickname. Nobody knows this but my birth name is John. There were 3 other kids by that name on the team, so I adopted that name just to stand out. The priest wouldn't Baptize me unless I was named after a saint."

Jacques asked: "If you would have known what he was going to do would you have supported him?"

Jasper said: "Yes. I would have helped."

Jacques said: "No more questions your honor."

Eric said: "You may step down Jasper. Ladies and gentlemen of the jury, the case is now finished. Tomorrow we will hear closing arguments and I will give you instructions. Have a good evening everybody."

The bailiff yelled: "ALL RISE!!" Everybody rose and left the courtroom.

CHAPTER 25

The next morning everybody came in on time and started court. Eric said: "Good morning everyone. Today we will start the closing arguments and then it will be off to deliberations. I will explain the procedure and instructions later on in the day. Charles, you may begin."

Charles said: "Thank you your honor. Ladies and gentlemen of the jury. I am going to give you the reasons why you should find him guilty. He already said he did it. The only question is how long he should spend in jail? I would say give him life because he spent a year knowing the family was waiting for word on where he is. He chose to torture the victim's family as well. He also chose to victimize another boy who moved away. He choise to victimize another boy and destry his life. He intimidated this boy by saying nothing. There is also no proof that the victim actually raped his sister. There is always the possibility that he killed the wrong person.

If he did this to one person he can do it to anybody. Nobody is safe. You have an obligation to keep the people of Boston safe. Do not turn your back on this part of the job. If you do let him go without jail hime he could come after you next. It could also be your family members. All because you let this animal out in the streets. Thank you all."

CHAPTER 26

Eric said: "Jacques, you may begin."

Jacques said: "Thank you your honor. Ladies and gentlemen of the jury. It is obvious he did it. It is also obvious that he had some kind of rage running through his veins for years. I urge you to find him guilty and sentince him to a mental hospital. He obviously has anger issues. Wouldn't you explode into a rage if you had experienced something like this? He need psychiatric help to deal with his blind rage, not jail time. It is obvious that something else happened to him as a young child that he held in all these years. He did tell me he was raped by relatives and never said anything. If anything he needs help redirecting his rage to more constructive means. Even if that means a rubber room or putting together jigsaw puzzles. You do have the right to sentence him to life in a mental institution, but he will not get the help he needs by rotting in a jail cell.

I call upon your Christian duty to reach out and help this troubled soul and not punish him. Thank you."

Eric said: "Ladies and gentlemen. You have now heard both sides of this argument. You must decide whether or not to find him guilty or not guilty by reason of mental disease or defect. Take your time with this decision. There is no hurry in coming to a decision. You will work until 3:00 and then return tomorrow if no decision is made. If you need a readback of any testimony send a note through the bailiff and I will send it in.

He will be posted outside to make sure you are not disturbed. Turn off your cell phones so that there are no distractions. Normally we don't allow them in negotiations, but if you give me your word you can keep it with you. You will appoint a foreperson of your choosing. This foreperson has the job of reading the verdict. You will now be escorted into the room and begin. Are there any questions?"

Everybody said: "No sir. You have our word that our cell phones won't go off."

With that everybody went into the other room to begin.

CHAPTER 27

They were all escorted into the room and sat down. The judge provided them with water and cookies. They were lucky to get that. As soon as they sat down somebody's cell phone rang off. That was against the judge's orders.

Juror number one said: "I don't buy the whole story of Jasper's being touched like that. I think he is just trying to get in the limelight and his fifteen minutes of fame."

Juror number two said: "I am not sure I could work for a guy like Jordan. He never smiles and is too serious. I would hate to sneeze in his presence."

Juror number three said: "I think that is just a façade for court. I wonder what he is really like in the office and at home."

Juror number four said: "He is probably a very nice and fun loving guy at home. He was the one who had the wisdom to call for outside help. Otherwise this city would still be in a heap of fear. It makes me thing maybe Las Vegas is the pace to live."

Juror number five said: "Your only knowledge of Las Vegas
is these four detectives who happened to solve the case
of this heinous act. It makes the Boston police look bad.
I personally would not mind having that John character
for a husband."

The chair person said: "Can we have a vote?"

They voted and it came down to 10 to convict and 2 to
acquit. There was a call out to ask who voted against
conviction. Juror number ten raised his hand and said he
thought Victor was not acting alone. He must have been
covering up for someone. Nobody agreed. Juror number
eleven said he just didn't look like the type. That was a load
of bologna anyway. He changed his vote just to get out of
there. Juror number 10 didn't want to be there either. He
also changed his vote just to get out of there. They sent a
note to the judge that they were ready.

The judge said: "We will read it tomorrow. Everybody go
home and get a good night's sleep. I promise it will not
be a full day tomorrow. Good night all."

The judge put the sealed envelope in the right hand drawer
of his desk. He locked it so that nobody knew what the
verdict was. The lawyers understood that nobody was
allowed to look at the verdict until it is read. The lawyers
never went against the wishes of the judge.

CHAPTER 28

The next day starte dout very badly. The judge came in and his office was turned upside down. It was obviously invaded and the envelope with the verdict was missing. All the bailiffs were questioned and the guilty party hadn't ben found. The judge called the jury to the courtroom. He had to ask the jury foreperson to repeat what was in the envelope. The gulty party was found and it was the defendant himself. He was found guilty, but sent to jail and he got life instead of time in a mental institution. He faced an extra five years for breaking and entering into the judge's chambers. Eric was glad to be rid of that defendant. He was put into isolation in jail and protective custody because of the heinous act of his crimes. He was killed in jail a month later despite all the protective custody. Somebody merely beat the tar out of him. The warden was relieved because he didn't want this person in his prison. Word got out of his crimes even before he whowed up. He was not in a position to deny the arrival of a prisoner.

CHAPTER 29

Norman got word that the case was closed and they were all free to go home. The day before they left Jordan took them all out to a steak house to toast new friends and new lessons learned. They were allowed to keep the sweatsuits they were given. Jordan even made friends with Commissioner the horse. As soon as John walked into the room the horse woke up and went into play mode. The three of them took a walk together along the grass. Commissioner really got excited and started neighing and becoming vocal and dancing around. They all bid each other farewell and departed for the last time.

The next day everybody checked out of the hotel by 9:00 and tried to make their way back to route 80 westbound. They took the same route as coming down only in the opposite direction. All the women stocked the RV's with fresh mild and bread and lunchmeat so that they didn't have to eat all three meals out. It took them seven days to drive back home to Nevada. They took their time.

There was really no hurry. John was on his best behavior all the way home. When they made it to Colorado Joyce called Ronald and Eloise to let them know they were almost home. Eloise insisted on making a turkey dinner to celebrate their return. They made it home by Saturday and somehow they made it to 5:00 Mass. There was a lot of handshaking and the priest said something to welcome them back. Daisy the Beagle dog even showed up. Everybody laughted hysterical when the two Great Danes pranced up the aisle. Robert apologized for their behaviour, but they hadn't been home yet.

Father Raaser said: "Good evening ladies and gentlemen. We are blessed to have the return of Robert Schapiro and his squad of detectives. They just came back from a trip to Boston to solve a cold case. Naturally they solved the case for them. We are fortunate to have their safe return."

The whole church exploded into applause. They were surprised to get home and see a refrigerator full of fresh food. That was compliments of Sr. Angelus. She went to John's house with her spare key. Father Raaser took Norman's house and Eloise took Robert's house. Everybody had spare keys for emergencies.

Norman got up and said: "Squad will return to work Monday morning. They didn't even get dressed on

Sunday. They all just laid around in the pajamas all day and got their rest.

Monday morning came and their first assignment was to return the RV's to the dealership. John reached out to return the horse to the stables.

On the following Sunday they made it to Ronald's house for their usual turkey dinner. There was much conversation and laughs around the table. Sr. Philomena was there to take it all in. They didn't leave until 6:00 in the night. All time got away from them once they got started.

The end.

Thank you to all my faithful readers. I will now start my 12th novel coming out maybe the end of this year. Following are excerps of my next novel.

The ANNIHALATION
of Police Officer JACK RHODES

CHAPTER 1

On May 1st, 2013 Las Vegas police officer Jack Rhodes was sitting in his kitchen having breakfast with his soon to be ex wife. He was in the throes of a very nasty divorce. They stayed together just for the sake of the children. His oldest daughter had just turned eighteen and according to the agreement between the two of them and the intervene person they all agreed to wait until their last child turned eighteen. He sat there and sulded behind the newspapter. His wife took him for all he had. Her biggest problem was that she overdid the credit cards and expected him to pay for everything. She never had any intentions to get a job. He felt better knowing he didn't have to pay child support. His wife always had oto buy the most expensive clothes for their kids and the most expensive groceries. She never did take to the idea of using coupons.

The lights went out suddenly and his wife told him to got check the fuse box. He did, but he didn't know what he was looking at. Everything looked normal to him. She took it as another opportunity to emasculate him and remind him of how stupid he was. When he didn't return she got up and went to look for him. She found him lying in a heap at the bottom of the stairs. Then it was lights out for her too. Somebody went after her with a bat to the head. Jack woke up and stumbled to the kitchen. He was bleeding profusely from the head. He tried to cover his wounds with a paper towel. It did no good

CHAPTER 2

He heard the doorbell ring and thought it was the ringing in his ears. He lost the power of speech and couldn't muster the energy to call out to come in. The door opened and in walks the real estate agent and the potential buyers. He forgot that was happening today. He vaguely heard voices from far away. He hoped that whomever it was wanted a cup of coffee. When he was found the real estate agent let out a blood curdling scream that would sterilize a squirrel three blocks away. The potential buyers stepped in and called emergency services for help. Johanna the agent knew that Jack was a cop, so she made the call to the sergeant. The buyers went to the basement and found Mrs. Rhodes lying in a heap at the bottom of the stairs. Unfortunately she was dead on impact. The emergency services came and carted Jack away. The coroner was called for Mrs. Rhodes. It took three hours to wrap up the whole scene.

CHAPTER 3

An ambulance was called for Jack. He coded in the ambulance, but the paramedics were able to bring him back. A neighbor called Norman to inform him of what just happened. Norman stormed the hospital hallways like his pants were on fire. Robert and his squad were already waiting at the hospital. John organized the group to line up against the walls so that they do not interfere with whom is a patient and whom was there for the cop. Norman was impressed by this show of leadership. He made a mental note of what John did. That was for another time. He was allowed to go into Jack's room and start talking to him.

Norman asked: "How are you feeling?"

Jack said: "Just a wee bit woozy sir."

Norman said: "That is to be expected. Do you remember what happened?

Jack said: "Last thing I remember I was sitting at the kitchen table and reading the paper and next thing it was lights out."

Norman asked: "Where were you when you woke up?"

Jack said: "I was in the kitchen, but I do not remember how I got there."

Norman asked: "Who found you?"

Jack said: "I am not sure. I remember the paramedics standing over me."

Norman asked: "Whom else did you see?"

Jack said: "There was a strange woman standing over me, but I couldn't for the life of me tell who she was, how she got there or why she was in my house."

Norman said: "Apparently your house is for sale. That strange woman was the real estate agent showing your house to prospective buyers."

Jack said: "Oh yeah. Now I remember."

Just then the nurse came in and said that Norman had to leave for the night because Jack needed his sleep. They walked out to the hallway together and the doctor stopped them with the MRI results. It didn't look good for Jack. He had suffered a massive brain injury.

Norman objected profusely and said: "Wait a second doc. I was just talking to him. He sounded coherent to me albeit just a little sleepy.

The doctor said: "Yes Norman he did. But the next 72 hours will tell us if he will tell us if there will be any long term effects. I have to operate tonight and relieve the pressure on his skull. It will take at least 6 hours to repair the damage. I must ask you to leave and go home now. You are listed as Jack's next of kin. You have my word on it that I will call you the minute I know something. For now you will just have to trust me to do my job."

Norman reluctantly left. Robert drove him home. It was going to be a sleepless night for both of them. They knew there was nothing to be done, but that didn't make it any easier.

Unfortunately Jack passed away peacefully in his sleep that night. It was now up to Norman to put together a cop's funeral. It was Jack's last request to donate his organs, but the autopsy showed he was in advanced kidney failure due to diabetes. It was doubtful if Jack ever knew what was happening. His body started to shut down one organ at a time. Robert had to guide Norman in who to call first and how to arrange the funeral. John came over to assist.

Norman said: "Robert, first thing I want to know from Ronald is that whether or not Jack knew he was sick. He owed it to his children to take care of himself.

Robert said: "I already talked to Ronald about that a few years ago. He said it was possible for that to happen. We shouldn't blame Jack for not taking care of himself."

John said: "Norman, just chalk it up to a lack of noticing. Diabetes is a very nasty disease that can disguise itself as other things. For now our focus has to be on getting him to a funeral home and putting together the funeral.

The nurse came in and asked: "Norman, what funeral home do you want to use?"

Robert said: "We have a standing account with Kelly funeral home over on Bay Avenue. Please transfer the body over there. We will be there this afternoon."

The nurse asked: "What about a priest to give him last rights?"

Robert said: "Call Father Raaser over at St. Mary's parish. He is the cop's counselor for murders."

Norman said: "This is now a cop's murder investigation. We will need to close this soon."

Robert said: "After we do the funeral my squad will begin working on it right away."

Norman said: "Tonight will be better. The sooner we start the sooner we can close this."

Robert said: "Let's get you to the funeral home first then take it to the next step."

They led him to the funeral home and it took 30 minutes from start to finish. He was cremated. The hardest part for Norman was picking out the coffin. Robert picked one out and Norman agreed to it. The coffin had to be burned with the body and the pillow, so the funeral home director cut down his choices by 2 as to which ones would burn. He promised Norman he would take care of the pillow and inner lining. There was a 3 hour waiting time for viewing the body. Amazingly there were no visible signs of a struggle or anything. He looked so natural that he looked like he had a heart attack. Norman was more upset about the diabetes issue that Jack had to live with. Robert called Ronald to come over and talk to Norman about the issue. That didn't make it any easier, but that evening before the gang left Norman made an order that everybody was to get tested for diabetes as soon as possible. The whole police squad had 30 days for a complete physical exam. Everybody yesed him to death. Everbody knew it was the grief talking.

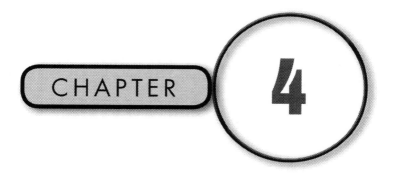

CHAPTER 4

The day of the funeral was a very difficult one for Norman. He was like a brother to him. He barely got through delivering the eulogy. John was a little sick to his stomach when he arrived at the crematory. It was surprising that he didn't see anything. All they did was to put flowers on the coffin and say some prayers. Then they left.

Norman said: "Robert, start your investigation tomorrow moring first thing. You have the full cooperation of the police department. Start with Jack's partner Carol. She is a woman all the way around."

Robert said: "Squad, tomorrow morning and 9:00 a.m. we will meet in my office for the first stages of the investigation."

Norman said: "POLICE DISMISSED!!!" They all saluted Jack one last time and exited the crematory.

Everybody went home in their own police cars. There was a caravan of 20 cars to exit the parking lot.